A BOOK ABOUT PRONOUNS

What ARE YOUR WORDS?

KATHERINE LOCKE · ILLUSTRATED BY ANNE PASSCHIER

Little, Brown and Company
New York Boston

My uncle Lior is coming to visit today! I can't wait to show them around my neighborhood. And I can't wait for all my neighbors to meet them!

Lior is my favorite uncle.

They have many beautiful, colorful hats.

The garden at their house is magical.

They are a biologist and look at teeny-tiny living things under a microscope.

I learn a lot from Uncle Lior, like that people can be described by more than what they look like or what they do. In fact, there are lots of words to say who people are and how they feel. Some of those words are pronouns. Pronouns are words that can take the place of your name, like *I*, *me*, *you*, *she*, *he*, or *they*.

Uncle Lior knows how important *my* words are to me because I am always growing and changing, and some of my words change with me. So every time they visit they ask, "What are your words, Ari?"

Sometimes I know my words right away.

HAPPY! CREATIVE!
FUNNY! HE/HIM

Sometimes I have to think about my words.

THOUGHTFUL! ATHLETIC!
SILLY! SHE/HER

Sometimes I have to try my words out.

SLEEPY! CALM!
HONEST! EY/EM

Sometimes I just use
one set of pronouns.

Sometimes I change
my pronouns.

Sometimes I use all the
pronouns I can think of.

My pronouns are like the weather. They change depending on how I feel.

AND THAT'S OKAY, BECAUSE THEY'RE MY WORDS.

This time when Uncle Lior asks about my words, I have a problem.

"I don't know what words to use!" I cry. I can't decide which pronouns fit today.

"That's okay," Uncle Lior tells me, their smile warm. "You have all day to think about it!"

But I want to know my words *now*.
He and *him* feel squirmy and wiggly to me.
Those aren't right.

I'll have to think about my words later because it's time for Uncle Lior, my sister, Rachel, and me to head to our neighborhood's big summer bash. Summer is my favorite season, and barbeques are my favorite type of party!

Rachel dances and sings in the street, twirling around and making me laugh. Rachel has her own words. Her pronouns don't change, but sometimes she's quiet instead of loud.

Today she is loud!

Mrs. Bolton walks behind us, laughing at her friend Charlie's joke. Mrs. Bolton's cat chases Charlie's little brown dog up and down the sidewalk. Mrs. Bolton and Charlie each have their own words too.

Our neighbor Anna tinkers with her car in the driveway. When I first met Anna, she had a different name and used different pronouns. But now she goes by Anna and uses *she* and *her* every day. She's my favorite neighbor.

"I'll be there soon!" she calls.

ARTISTIC! SWEET! KIND! ZE/ZIR

We see Robin Day and zir kids drawing with chalk.

When I introduce Robin to Uncle Lior, I use zir words.

Uncle Lior says hello and tells zir their words too.

"We'll see you at the bash!" they say.

Ava and George from the ivy-covered house are on their way to the summer bash.

"Nice to meet you, Lior!" Ava says.

"They are *Uncle* Lior," I explain proudly. Everyone laughs. Rachel laughs the loudest and turns to me.

"What are your words today, Ari?" she asks.

I think about my words.

She and *her* feel sharp and crackly to me.

Those won't work today.

WHY CAN'T I FIGURE OUT WHICH WORDS TO USE?

I WANT TO BE ABLE TO SHARE THEM WITH EVERYONE.

When we arrive at the bash, we see our new neighbor.

"Hello! My name is Ari. What are your words?" I ask.

"Hi, Ari! I'm Avery, and I use *they* and *them*," they reply.

"Like my uncle Lior!" I say. "What are your other words?"

Avery thinks. "My other words are *teacher*, *friendly*, and *loyal*! What are *your* words?" Avery asks.

I scrunch my face. I thought I would know by now.
"I'm not sure what fits me today," I tell them.

TEACHER! FRIENDLY!
LOYAL!
THEY/THEM

I try out some other words.
Ey and *eir* feel heavy and bumpy to me.
Those don't fit either!

"You'll figure it out," Avery tells me. "Sometimes it just takes patience."

But I don't want to be patient. It shouldn't take this long to find my words.
Everyone else seems to know theirs!

I go to Uncle Lior and tug on their sleeve. "I still don't know my words."

"That's okay," Uncle Lior says reassuringly. "They're your words.
They didn't disappear. If you don't know them today, you'll know
them tomorrow."

Soon, it's time for fireworks. I wait for the show to start,
just like I've been waiting all day to figure out my words.
Waiting makes me buzzy like a bee and makes my skin feel itchy.
When the first explosions finally burst in the sky, everyone gasps.
Suddenly I feel my words fall into place.

Sometimes I know my words right away.

Sometimes I have to think about my words.

Sometimes I have to try my words out.

But sometimes I have to wait for my words to find me.

I squeeze Uncle Lior's hand.

"Uncle Lior!" I whisper excitedly.

"What?" they ask.

There's another boom of fireworks, and colors race through the sky.

I point. "Those are my words! I'm like fireworks!

IMPATIENT!
EXCITED!
COLORFUL!

And *they* and *them* feel right today."

"Fireworks!" Uncle Lior says with a laugh.
They squeeze my hand back. "That's
definitely you, Ari."

My words finally found me!
They and *them* feel warm and snug to me.
These pronouns are perfect.

CONFIDENT

CURIOUS

XE/XIR

GENEROUS

KIND

ZE/ZIR

MECHANIC

NEIGHBOR

HE/HIM RESPONSIBLE

SHE/HER

When the fireworks are over, we walk home, all our words floating with us.

And our pronouns too.

THEY/THEM

SISTER   EY/EM

GARDENER

TEACHER

HAPPY

Hi there! I haven't met you yet.
My name is Ari. My words are *impatient*, *bouncy*,
excited, *nervous*, *colorful*, and *hopeful*.
And today my pronouns are *they* and *them*.

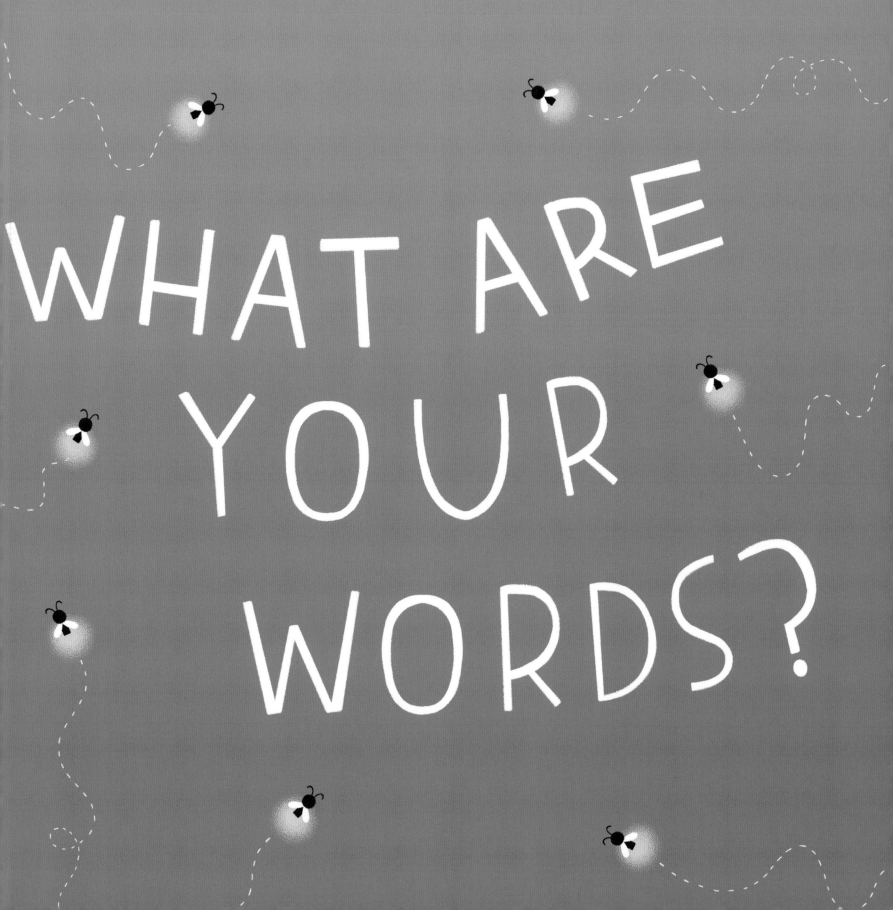

Author's Note

This book is about pronouns! Pronouns may or may not indicate someone's gender. Someone who uses *he/him* may be agender or nonbinary, for example. Just as it is important to not make assumptions about what people's words are, it is important to not make assumptions about people's gender based on their pronouns or their presentation. You can find more resources at mypronouns.org and GLSEN.org.

———————

For you, if you're still finding your words. –KL

To anyone who needs it: your words are valid, they are true, and they are yours. –AP

———————

About This Book

The illustrations for this book were done digitally. This book was edited by Regan Winter and designed by Sasha Illingworth. The production was supervised by Lillian Sun, and the production editor was Annie McDonnell. The text was set in Minou Regular, and the display type is hand-lettered.